CAMP CREEPY

#5 The Return
of the
Color War Ghost

Written by
Laurie Friedman

Illustrated by
Jake Hill

A LEAVES CHAPTER BOOK

CRABTREE
Publishing Company
www.crabtreebooks.com

Dear Caregiver/Teacher,

Leaves Chapter Books will engage readers immediately by grabbing their attention with exciting plots, adventurous characters, and amazing illustrations. Each series is carefully designed to provide students with reading skills and knowledge to become confident readers. Students will take pleasure in reading and enjoy the adventure it takes them on. These books can be used for independent or shared reading.

School-to-Home Support for Caregivers and Teachers

This book helps children grow by letting them practice reading. Here are a few guiding questions to help the reader with building his or her comprehension skills. Possible answers appear here in red.

Before Reading:
- What do I think this story will be about?
  - *I think this story will be about ghosts that scare the campers while they play games outside.*
  - *I think this story will have scary places where the ghosts hide.*

During Reading:
- Pause and look at the words and pictures. Why did the character do that?
  - *I think the campers cheered for their teammates to help them win.*
  - *I think Will knew he had to come up with a solution during the tug-of-war if the campers were going to beat the stronger ghosts.*

After Reading:
- Describe your favorite part of the story.
  - *My favorite part was when the campers shouted "BLUE MOON."*
  - *I liked seeing the ghosts fall into the quicksand pit with the snakes.*

TABLE OF CONTENTS

CAMP CREEPY LAKE

THE CAMP CREEPY LAKE CURSE

Once upon a time, there was a camp on the shores of pretty Sleepy Lake.

Camp Sleepy Lake.

Kids loved coming to the camp. They were good kids.

Counselors loved working at the camp. They loved the good kids.

But one summer, the kids were not good. They were BAD.

So that summer, the counselors took matters into their own hands.

They hired a witch. She put a curse on the camp.

Camp Sleepy Lake became Camp Creepy Lake.

The goal of the camp: SCARE BAD KIDS!

To be fair, not all kids who came to the camp were bad.

But it didn't matter. The curse couldn't tell a good kid from a bad kid.

So from that day forth, ALL campers who attended the camp were cursed.

And no campers ever returned to Camp Creepy Lake for a second summer.

Chapter 1
Red vs. Blue

Will's tummy rumbled. Today's lunch . . . chicken wings. With the feathers still on them! Will looked around the table. Not one other boy in Bunk Five had eaten a bite.

Strange food was just one of the many creepy things about Camp Creepy Lake.

There were lots of others.

Bones, their counselor, was a real skeleton. A wicked witch ran the waterfront. Big, growling dogs followed campers everywhere they went.

Every day at Camp Creepy Lake was a new and SCARY experience!

When lunch was over, Old Donny stood in front of the campers.

Just the sight of the pale, ghostlike camp director with the long, white beard scared the campers. Silence fell over the room.

"I have an announcement to make," said Old Donny.

"This can't be good," Will whispered to his best friend, Chase.

"No way," said Chase. Old Donny never had anything good to say.

"Tomorrow is a special day at Camp Creepy Lake. We're having a color war! Red team versus the blue team." Old Donny flashed a pleasant smile.

The dining hall filled with the sounds of cheering kids. Will pushed his glasses up on his nose. Old Donny rarely smiled. And never in a pleasant way.

"Weird," Will mumbled out loud.

Old Donny waited until the dining hall was quiet. "Tomorrow at breakfast, you'll be assigned to teams and given T-shirts. Then the color war games will begin."

"About time we get to do something like kids at normal camps!" said Chase.

The boys in Bunk Five high-fived each other. They got what Chase meant. Camp Creepy Lake was definitely NOT a normal camp.

Will was quiet while the other boys in Bunk Five—Chase, Alex, Jake, Max, and Tony—talked about the color war. They were excited. But Will had a bad feeling he couldn't shake.

Chapter 2
New Teams

The next morning, Will walked into the dining hall and smelled burnt toast.

Nothing unusual about that. But then he saw something that scared him. And every other camper too.

"Sit down!" hissed Old Donny.

Kids scrambled to find their seats. They sat, staring at a creepy, ghostlike team of counselors lined up across the front of the dining hall. They were wearing Camp Creepy Lake T-shirts, gym shorts, and sneakers, and flexing their oversized muscles.

"Do you recognize any of them?" Will asked Chase.

"Not a one," Chase whispered back.

"They look like body builders," said Tony.

"Shut up!" hissed Bones. "Old Donny has something to say."

The director of Camp Creepy Lake stood in front of them. "There's been a change of plans," he announced.

His lip curled into an evil sneer. "There will not be a red team and blue team. Instead, campers will compete against old counselors." Old Donny's voice was low and scary. "The ghosts of past color wars have returned. And they want revenge."

Bones cupped his bony hands over his mouth and shouted

to Old Donny. "Tell them what happens to the losing team."

Old Donny laughed. A deep, scary belly laugh. Bones joined in. So did Maude, Old Donny's weird wife. And other staffers too. No Name, the creepy activities director. Fang, the weird head of the craft shop. And Bam, the archery teacher who looked like Frankenstein.

Staff and counselors were all belly-laughing like the idea of what would happen to the losing team filled them with glee.

"WHOA!" said Chase. "This is bad."

"Very bad!" mumbled Will.

Chapter 3
Let the Games Begin!

The first event of the color war was a three-legged race. Campers and ghosts running in it tied their feet together, then lined up.

"Ready. Set. Go!" No Name fired a starter pistol.

The runners took off down the field. Campers who weren't running cheered for their teammates.

Ghosts who weren't running lounged in chairs like they didn't need to cheer because they knew they'd win.

"Run, Nelly!" Chase and Will yelled to their good friend.

But Nelly and her partner, Sophie, quickly fell behind. The ghosts were so much faster.

The next set of campers fell further behind. And it just got worse from there. Campers cheered for their teammates. But it didn't help. The race ended. The ghosts won.

"We won't give up!" cheered the campers as they walked

to the waterfront for the next
round of events.

The ghosts were not good at
diving, and the campers easily
won the diving contest.

But the ghosts were strong swimmers. They won all of the swim relays, and the sailing and canoe races too.

After lunch, everyone met on the soccer field for the afternoon events.

The Camp Creepy Lake campers put their arms around each other. They did a loud team cheer. Their spirits were high as they won the sing-off and the fire-building contest. But the ghosts cheered just as loudly when they won the soccer match and basketball game.

The scoreboard showed that the ghosts were ahead—100 to 75.

"We won't give up!" the campers yelled as they marched together to the archery field for

the final afternoon events.

They cheered like crazy when they won the dance-a-thon.

But they were no match for the strong ghosts, and lost the ax throw, the hatchet hunt, and the archery shootout.

The afternoon events ended. The score for the day: ghosts—125, campers—100.

"We won't give up!" cheered the campers as they marched to the dining hall.

At dinner, the ghosts were served steak and baked potatoes. Campers got frozen pizza. That was still frozen!

"We won't give up!" they chanted as Old Donny stood to make an announcement.

"Tonight is the final event— the tug-of-war. It's worth 50 points." His eyes narrowed as he looked at the campers in the dining hall.

"Losers, beware!"

"What do you think happens to the losers?" Chase asked the boys of Bunk Five.

They all shivered. None of them wanted to find out.

Chapter 4
Tug-of-War

The Sun was starting to set. Fire torches were lit. The campers walked out onto the field for the final event of the day—the tug-of-war.

A thick rope stretched across a large pit filled with a dark, gritty substance. Old Donny and Maude were seated on a raised platform. They looked down at the pit, smiling evil smiles.

The campers gasped.

"Is that mud?" Chase mumbled.

"Quicksand," said Will. "I'm pretty sure it's quicksand. But it's not as bad as it looks. It's rare to die in quicksand."

Jake pointed to something moving in the pit.

"Snakes!" screamed Tony as a whole army of them rose to the surface.

Campers muttered and moaned in disbelief. The girls in Bunk Two started to cry.

The staff was laughing, as though they were enjoying the reaction of the campers.

Will's mouth dropped open. But no sound came out. Maybe they could survive the quicksand. But not the snakes!

Then the ghosts sprinted out onto the field. They flexed their big muscles. All of them looked ready to battle.

"Campers, line up and grab the rope," said Old Donny.

No Name began to herd the campers into line.

Nelly's hands shook as she grabbed on to the thick rope.

"Holy moly! We're going to end up in that pit!" she whispered to Will and Chase.

"We're no match for those ghosts!" Chase's voice trembled as he spoke.

A knot of fear formed in Will's throat. His friends were right. They couldn't beat the ghosts with strength. But there had to be some other way to win the tug-of-war.

The problem was . . . Will had no clue what it might be.

Chapter 5
Moonlight Madness

No Name raised his starter pistol. He fired it into the air.

The ghosts began to tug on the rope. The campers tugged back. They tugged hard. But it didn't help. They were quickly being pulled toward the pit.

"We have to do something!" yelled Chase "And fast!"

"It's hard to think and pull," said Will. His brain raced with thoughts. He glanced up at the moon in the night sky. An idea suddenly came to him.

"Blue moon!" said Will to Chase. "On the count of three, we'll all yell blue moon."

Chase shook his head. "But the moon isn't blue."

"Doesn't matter," said Will. "The ghosts will look to see if it is. When they get distracted, we pull and win."

"We don't have much time!" said Chase. The ghosts were pulling the campers closer and closer to the edge of the pit.

"Spread the word. And fast!" said Will.

He and Chase told his idea to the kids in front of them and behind them. The idea quickly made its way to all of the campers.

"ONE. TWO. THREE!" shouted Will.

Then the voices of the campers rang out as one. "BLUE MOON!" they yelled.

The ghosts stopped pulling and looked up.

"PULL!" yelled Will.

The campers pulled with all of their strength. The ghosts of color wars past screeched as they all tumbled forward into the pit.

"We did it!" cried Chase.

The boys of Bunk Five looped their arms around each other and did a victory dance. All of the Creepy Lake campers joined in the cheering.

Old Donny stood frozen on the platform until the loud cheering stopped.

"Campers win the color war," he announced. Then Old Donny's eyes narrowed. He cleared his throat and spoke words no campers would forget.

"Everything at Camp Creepy Lake is about to change. Absolutely everything."

ABOUT THE AUTHOR

Laurie Friedman is the award-winning author of more than seventy-five critically acclaimed picture books, chapter books, and novels for young readers, including the bestselling *Mallory McDonald* series and the *Love, Ruby Valentine* series. She is a native Arkansan, and in addition to writing, loves to read, bake, do yoga, and spend time with her friends and family. For more information about Laurie and her books, please visit her website at www.lauriebfriedman.com.

ABOUT THE ILLUSTRATOR

Jake Hill grew up in North London, but escaped to the South Coast to study illustration and decided to stay by the sea, swimming (almost) every morning! Aside from his love of drawing, Jake is an avid reader, a meticulous collector of comics, a terrible, but improving, pianist, and a passionate player of games. There are few things Jake enjoys as much as walking in the fresh air of Exmoor National Park.

CRABTREE
Publishing Company

Written by: Laurie Friedman
Illustrations by: Jake Hill
Art direction and layout by: Rhea Wallace

Series Development: James Earley
Proofreader: Melissa Boyce
Educational Consultant: Marie Lemke M.Ed.

Library and Archives Canada Cataloguing in Publication

CIP available at Library and Archives Canada

Library of Congress Cataloging-in-Publication Data

CIP available at Library of Congress

Crabtree Publishing Company
www.crabtreebooks.com   1-800-387-7650

Printed in the U.S.A./CG20210915/012022

Published in the United States
Crabtree Publishing
347 Fifth Avenue, Suite 1402-145
New York, NY, 10016

Published in Canada
Crabtree Publishing
616 Welland Ave.
St. Catharines, ON, L2M 5V6